SINGLE **SISTER,** SINGLE **MOTHER**

I AM MANDIRA

SURESH THADHANI

notionpress.com

INDIA • SINGAPORE • MALAYSIA

ISBN
Paperback 979-8-89777-496-8
Hardcase 979-8-89777-497-5

Dedications:

*My sincere dedications to my loyal family, without their help and support even a shadow of this book would not be a look for the **reader**!*

Acknowledgements

My grateful acknowledgements to Publishers and their Team for turning my manuscripts into full-fledged books.

HAPPY READING!

STAY SAFE HEALTHY AND BLESSED.

About the Author

The Author is a mature person who is based in Dubai for the past four and a half decades. He is originally from Bombay (now) Mumbai, India. Writing is his forte and he has done quite a few stints in college magazines and social clubs. He has visited many countries, on the six continents, and loves travelling. Many of his stories are based on real time episodes and he churns them out interestingly in a witty way, easy to understand and bringing a smile on readers' lips. In his own words, he says, if I cannot make you laugh in the first five minutes, then I will cry! Interestingly he adds, and as you are a good person, you don't' want me to cry! So, there you go smiling. His core career is based in the accounting field, but he says he wants to be in the field and so has quit accounting!

He believes all of us on this Good Planet are Students of Life, and likewise we too need to be Good in Life too!

Single Sister, Single Mother

is a witty story that shadows loneliness and weaves its own charming happiness. A sister and a brother Mandira and Ankesh, are living alone in a big city of Mumbai — their unparallel love for each other makes their lives easy despite their parents living overseas. Mandira is a champion in sports and has more credits in her sports life than in her routine college and office life. With her sheer guts and integrity, she rises to be a Fitness Instructor, managing household affairs, playing a motherly and sisterly role in her day-to-day life. Their silent mischief and tease-pull-jokes leave you thrilling. Sudesh, the Boss's son, is charmed by Mandira — but she has other plans and is married to Sports. Glances exchange, but not sports.

Author Suresh Thadhani

Table of Contents

Characters in the Story

ANKY: THE STORY TELLER

MANDIRA: (FONDLY CALLED AS MANDY) ELDER SISTER OF ANKESH

JERRY SIMON: UNCLE OF MANDIRA & ANKESH

SHERRY: DAUGHTER OF JERRY SIMON

PARENTS OF MANDIRA & ANKESH: JEROME & JANET WORKING IN KUWAIT

CLASSMATES: CATHY, GILBERT, DANIEL, HARRY, KENNY, MEERA

CLASS TEACHERS: SAM TIMOTHY, MRS. SHEEREN FATIMA, JOLINE PERERIA

ROLAND: BROTHER OF CATHY

MANDIRA'S FRIENDS: JEMIMA, YASIN, AMINA

K CLUB: POPULAR SPORTS CLUB IN BANDRA BANDSTAND, MUMBAI

AMRITLAL SHAH: OWNER OF JANATA IMPORTS
AND EXPORTS

SUDESH SHAH: SON OF AMRITLAL

AND OTHERS: RATAN LAL, SHRI KANT, PAWAR
EMPLOYEES OF JANATA IMPORTS AND EXPORTS

Chapter 1

The Yoga Session

Mandira got up from the floor, uncrossing her legs, stood up without any shake up and stood still for a moment. She quietly balanced herself in a TREE POSTURE, closing her eyes. Satisfied, she could stand on one leg clasping her two hands above her head without any jerks, she changed to the other leg following the same procedure. Then she closed her eyes and prayed, thanking Lord Budha. This was her daily yoga sessions.

She heard the clock strike six times and was satisfied her forty-five minutes of yoga was gainfully complied with. This was an oath her mother, Janet, had given to her to practice daily when she was just five years old. Mandira had religiously followed her regime. Later, from the age of ten, she had enrolled herself in marshal art training, vowing to be a gold medalist in every sport she would compete. Today was her birthday and she was turning Sweet Eighteen!

Thoughts running down her mind, she entered the kitchen to make a simple breakfast for herself and her younger brother, Ankesh. She knew her younger brother would get up by 7am and she still had a margin of time to do her other household jobs. Just for a stunt she ran forward and jumped high up in the air trying to touch the light bulb which was about ten feet higher than the floor. The bulb missed her beatings by an inch or so, oscillated a little left and right with the force of Mandira's hand sweeping. She was pleased with her stunt thanking God the bulb swayed only a little wayward and nothing untoward happened.

The hard tapings of her footsteps were a sure sign for Ankesh to get up soon. Though Ankesh mentally protested, he knew he would have to get up and go to school. Around 7am his school bus would come, and he had an hour to get ready. Sleepily he got up, grabbed his towel behind his room door, and went to the bathroom. For some unknown reason, Ankesh enjoyed bathroom singing at the top of his voice. He knew Mandira would be angry and waited for her to yell at him and then he would lower his voice but continue singing. "Anky, lower your high-pitched volume, the song will still be fine" Mandira shouted from the kitchen. Happy at the yell and a little appreciation from Mandira, Ankesh softened his voice, now almost a whisper, and after 8 minutes came out of the bathroom, with a bath towel wrapped around his waist, fresh, and beaming, he ran to the house temple and prayed to Lord Budha's statue preserved on a small fountain. Prayers over, he rushed to the kitchen and called out "Mandy, what is the breakfast you made today for me?" Ankesh always called Mandira by her pet name: Mandy. Likewise, Mandira called her brother "Anky" instead of Ankesh. "Oh! I forgot, Happy, Happy, Birthday to you, my dearest Mandy and he hugged her kissing her cheeks, one at a time and continuing "Happy, Happy Birthday to my dearest, dearest sister. He lifted her off the ground and swayed her in his arms saying "You are eighteen now, and I am only twelve, when will I become eighteen? Big, Strong and Bold like you?

"Okay, my sweet pie, put me on the ground, I have a *mandira* (a churning wooden stick with six bulb like cloves: a kitchen mashing utensil) in my hand. "OK" down you go, and he dropped her with a *"thud"* releasing her bit by bit till her feet reached the floor. "And what is my breakfast, anything special on your s-p-e-c-i-a-l day! "Yes, dearie, you have an omelet without an egg" and plain untoasted bread to go along with it" she giggled. "Yes, I shall have it, because today is your cooking day and mine will be tomorrow ...." Be Prepared" Ankesh replied, a scout's motto. Both laughed, sister and brother teasing each other. Birthday was a funday, and Ankesh mischievously spread a little milk powder on her cheeks, and once again cried "Happy Birthday "Mandira dusted milk powder on her tongue and then kissed her brother's forehead. Ankesh cheerfully wiped it with a tissue and sat down on the chair for his breakfast. Mandira brought out a big brown Brownie splattered with colorful smarties and handed it to her brother. "Take this special treat as breakfast" for my birthday, and she lowered the plate to Ankesh's mouth. Astonished with the sudden turnout of the events, Ankesh respectfully pulled his sister to the plate and said both of us will eat the Brownie, with me taking a selfie! What a joy it is! We shall send these photos to our mum and dad in Kuwait!

"Mandy, I shall bring a gift for you in the evening, after school, as you too will also be returning by that time". It is OK with me, his sister replied. But you see that you don't spend too much on the gift, Mandira replied. She poured coffee for her brother and for herself, taking a piece of Brownie along with it. Happily, the brother and sister relished their breakfast. Ankesh told her sister to leave for her morning college. He would clean up the few dishes and go down for the school bus--- in about 15 minutes' time. Mandy was already ready to go and bade "Bye" to her brother. He waved his hand to her and she left pulling the door behind her.

Ankesh dressed up, wearing his school uniform: navy blue half pants, a white shirt, and an off brown tie. He looked into the dressing mirror, poked his tongue out, and mischievously whistled at his reflection. Deliberately, he pulled a streak of his hair to his forehead, making a "J" out of it for no reason. Again, he looked into the mirror and slowly moved out of the room and closed the door behind him ensuring he had the door key in the right hand.

Chapter 2

Birthday Gift for Mandy

The school bus was just turning from the side lane, when I hoped out from the staircase. All the other children had lined up for the school bus, some with their moms, some with their house keepers, and still others with none, like me. The conductor moved us, one by one, taking care to hold our arm, if at all we stumbled, or looked back to wave at our caretakers. My parents were in Kuwait, and I had a faint memory of them leaving me this way, in the good old times, may be six years back. Now it was my Mandy who took care of me: Like my mom, my aunties, or anybody who stayed with us for some time. I did not know what poverty was, but only remember Mandy told me, "Our parents have to earn aboard" to give us a better standard of life, a terminology I did not understand then and even now! Though I remembered my parents in a distant way (they left for Kuwait when I was six years old, Mandy told me so).

The driver had a keen sense of observation and remembered every student's name – except mine--- he called me "Hero". And always I remembered my last glance in the mirror before leaving the house. Johnny, my classmate, came and sat next to me and shook hands, a gesture I was shy to do with girl students, but others did. There was noise in the bus and the conductor kept on shouting at us "Keep quiet" but still somehow or other, there was noise: the roar of the bus, children shouting or getting agitated due to window seats being unavailable.

The school was a better place, the class work boring, and the only time was comfortable was recess time : we could mix and match, play games, run here and there, eat from anyone and share our lunch boxes, go to loo, write on walls, though indiscreetly, and we drew heart signs, crosses, facial drawings , or anything that came in our minds. But all these adventures were hated by school staff who would question us: who did it? And periodically someone would be punished on suspected charges. As the bus slowed down near our school compound, I noticed the sports shop: MAXWELL SPORTS STUDIO--- this was the shop I was craning my neck to look at ---- I would be buying boxing gloves for Mandy.

At lunch time, I skipped slowly through the back gate of the school and crossed the busy road and went into the sports shop. "How much are these boxing gloves; I asked the sales attendant? IRS2000, the sales guy replied feeling in his mind I was not the right customer to buy this product. "OK, I shall buy it, any discount you can give, please? "I inquired. "for whom do you want to buy, as this is not for you, it is for ladies" the sales guy responded. "Yes, you are right, I want for my sister" I replied. "OK, you can have it and shall give you some discount---- pay me IRS1600 as you are my first customer today, the salesguy said. Quickly, I made the deal and asked for a paper bag to carry the gloves. Satisfied, I rushed back to the school, needing to put the gloves in my school bag, without anyone in the class noticing it. It was just a matter of 2 hours more for the class to end and I would surprise Mandy with my gift.

Reaching home, I decided to wrap the gloves in the given bag, with another bag so Mandy keeps on guessing the contents! I changed my school uniform, washed my face, had some biscuits and chips and was waiting for the knock on the door.

Going to my room, I found a Big Mac with fries on my desk. Surely, Mandy had a treat for me—she loved me as much as I loved her. Though our parents were abroad, we never felt lost in loneliness as we had vowed to always respect each other. Her friends came to our place, and we always enjoyed together, though I rarely invited my friends to our home. Where was Mandy, I wondered, if the burger was here, she too should have been here. I touched the fries, they were a little hot, meaning Mandy would be in the house or just outside. Then I heard a squeak and found her laughing in the kitchen. "Anky, you forgot to move the kitchen curtain, I was just behind it, but I saw you rush to your room, so I hid myself to give you a surprise. We hugged, we laughed, we cuddled, and suddenly I told Mandy "did you see me gift wrapping your gift: Ok, let me bring it to you: And guess what it is ? "I have no idea but feeling the gift with my hands, I think it is a soft toy! And she gently tore the wrapper and yelled "Boxing Gloves! The real thing I needed, as I am into Boxing practice now, and she wore at once and punched the wall. "Good, my fingers did not hurt, it is a great gift" very thoughtful of you and she kissed my forehead. I licked the tip of her nose and there we began running in the house----settling near the Big Mac.

My cell phone rang, and it was Uncle Jerry online. "Hello, dearie, you at home? "Yes, very much", Uncle, I politely replied. "Then, I shall be in a few minutes at your place, See You" Jerry replied and cut off. I called "Mandy, Uncle Jerry is coming here in a few minutes, I think he knows it is your birthday today. "Yes, he is welcome," my sister said. And we both dabbed our faces to look neat and clean. Uncle Jerry happened to be our Mum's cousin and was quite fond of us, at times he did drop in at our place, bringing a lot of goodies. Uncle Jerry was a retired judge having experience of over forty years in legal matters. He was rich and quite an influential person. It was he who had got jobs to our parents in Kuwait. He was well connected with wealthy Arabs in Kuwait who had oil refineries. We were sure he would be bringing a gift for Mandy today.

Soon there was a knock on the door, and we eagerly ran to the front door to welcome Uncle Jerry. "Hello, young lad, Ankesh, how are you? "I am good sir, please come in, and be comfortable with us. Uncle gave me a little pat on my cheek, and upon seeing Mandy in the doorway, happily cried "Happy Birthday to our dear Princesses, M-a-n-d-i-r-a, handing her a large bouquet of flowers and a small gift box.

Oh! Thank You Uncle, very kind of you to remember my birthday, and Thanks again, for the nice gift--- I am going to open right now to see what my favorite uncle has brought for me! saying this, she neatly opened the gift box. "A lovely watch, Oh! How nice, and I like the black dial with golden hands... oh so pretty, Thanks again. I peeped over the watch and liked it immensely; it was a pretty Casio watch with a nice round dial and star-like numbers with golden hands moving lazily under the glass. It looked pretty on Mandy's wrist--- I tied the watch on her wrist. "Why did you not bring, Sherry, your daughter along? Mandy asked Uncle Jerry; "Sherry, was not feeling so well, had a bit of a cough too, and did not want to come along, so I came alone. "Any news from Jerome and Janet, your parents: when are they coming down to Mumbai, any idea? Uncle Jerry asked politely. "Probably during Christmas time" Mandy ventured and added "Let us have coffee together, Uncle Jerry"

Sorry about that, I must leave now, as Sherry is alone replied Uncle. Okay just give me a glass of water, if you don't mind. "Yes, sure, and have this piece of my birthday cake, for you and Sherry" and Mandy gave Uncle, wrapping the cake pieces in a foil container. Before I leave, Uncle Jerry said "Please join us on Saturday evening at "Hotel Marriot near Bandstand, Bandra West "to celebrate your birthday postdate. Sherry and I have made bookings & we meet at 7pm. Shall also drop you at home, after dinner. "Thank You, Uncle, sure we both will join you at Marriot near Bandstand, Bandra. Thank You so much, Good Night" "Cheers" Uncle replied. "See you both on Saturday" and left towards his car.

"Mandy, tomorrow is my turn to make breakfast, anything special you need. I asked my sister; else I shall make my usual sandwiches. "It is OK with me, and we bade goodnight and went to sleep, excited with Uncle's visit and his gift. Mandy went to her room, carrying the gloves as well as the Casio watch. I could feel her excitement and of course, we were remembering our parents too! We could feel their blessings vibrating in our house!

Chapter 3

Gloves Utilised

It was just 5.30 AM in the morning and I could hear Mandy's prancing abouts in the kitchen. She was like, summersaulting and kicking the wall, bouncing back and again activating herself, with a sound like "Ho-Ho". Then there was a different sound: I could feel she was boxing wearing gloves and punching a gunny bag full of sand. I could often hear her shouts of woo-woo and what not. Though my sleep got disturbed, I was not the one to complain. I loved Mandy too much and would always think of her first--- even before my mum. The bond was so special that I cannot fully express it. My Mom and Dad were at a distance, and the closest person in the world was my loving sister, Mandira--- I called her Mandy for a different reason. My mother, makes delicious dishes, using queer kitchen utensils, a churning utensil called *Mandira* (a churning and mashing kitchen utensil) by which she used to make Sweet *Lassi* (Butter milk). Mandira used to dance round and round, my mom lovingly called her Mandira: and the name stuck. I fine-tuned her name to Mandy. Shaking my head a little, I turned my head on the pillow to get more sleep for some more time.

It was around 6am that I heard a loud thud. Then another followed. Rubbing my eyes, I came out of my room to see what was happening. I knew it would be Mandy. She was wearing gloves and practicing boxing on a sack full of old newspapers. Then she did another stunt – she ran towards the kitchen wall with full force, jumped up in the air, hit her both feet on the wall and pushed herself back with force and stood up straight like a soldier. This was a new stunt she was practicing for judo or karate practice I don't know. I watched in awe as she did this stunt three times, without baiting her eyelids. I clapped in delight noticing her perfect deadlock kick. "Mandy, how can you do such stunts fearlessly? "Concentration. Concentration", she replied with heavy breathing. Thank God, I did not get distracted by your presence, though I felt I did hear some footsteps and randomly guessed it could only be you. I smiled and disappeared into the washroom.

I managed to cut tomatoes, cucumbers, carrots, cabbage, white onions, boiled potatoes for vegetable sandwiches. Lightly, I toasted the bread slices in the griller, applied butter, put in the ingredients, making a double decker sandwich. I knew Mandy would relish the sandwich and crave more. There was a ring on the door, and I was wondering who could be so early? Before I could reach the door, Mandy had opened the door and saw a postman delivering her an envelope. "You Mandira "? Here is a courier addressed to you, from Kuwait. My sister almost jumped at receiving the courier post --- she had guessed it was a gift for her birthday, from Mom & Dad! And she was right – but there was a problem: The courier guy, facing Mandy with boxing gloves, was puzzled and thought she would jab him a blow: so, he too was standing with fighter's pose with two fists drawn. Mandy laughed and replied she was self-practicing boxing. The courier guy apologized and said he came very early, as he missed the delivery schedule yesterday, and was quite apologetic and left smiling, wishing her a renewed Good Morning! Mandy opened the courier packaging and kissing the envelope she pulled out an Eighteen Thousand Rupees Bank Transfer Advice from Mom & Day, written with a note "Very Happy Birthday to my

Sweetie, Darling Mandira. Enjoy Your Day with Ankesh Baba (I was still a Baba—a child -- to my mom, as she often lovingly called me). We were both very happy and Thanked Mama and Papa, whistling in the air, "Thank You, Mom & Dad, Thank You, Thank You So Much"

The striking clock at 6AM brought us to our senses, and we rushed to finish our morning chores. I could feel the oncoming summer heat even at 6AM and rushed to bathe. Mandy too had rushed for bath, after folding neatly her gift envelope at the feet of Lord Budha. This was our upbringing: Always Thank the Lord for everything happening in our life. It is the Lord's wish. So be it!

Mandy ate the sandwich lovingly, often glancing at me and teasing "Encore, Encore" I beamed and showed her my two thumbs. I rushed back to finish kitchen chores and get ready for the school bus to come. In the nick of the time, I reached down and saw the school bus just turning in and halting below our building. There were smaller kids who wanted to jump in the bus, earlier than everyone and choose a window seat. I always was the last to hop on the bus as I wouldn't care wherever I got the seat, I would make myself comfortable. Unfortunately, today I got a seat next to Cathy, and she fondly touched my arm, much to my disappointment. She politely asked "Are you Mandira's brother? ""if you know it, why do you ask? I curtly replied. She was a bit taken back, but boldly replied "I did not mean any offence, just wanted to confirm, as I have often seen you in the park, as I too live in the same compound: Pali Hill Compound. "Oh, yes, I now understand," I replied. So, Rodney, is your brother? Does he also attend The K Club, like my sister does? "Yes", hence I asked you ---- Is Mandira your sister? Realizing the truth of her sentence, I smiled at her, and in turn she beamed and shook hands with me "Pleased to meet you, I am Cathy Vaz". "And as you now know me, I am Ankesh" The school bus stopped. All got down, me holding her hand, she shyly looking at other children looking at us. For the first time in my life, I had held a girl's hand, and I felt unsure of my feelings. Anyway, I shall tell Mandy about this new friendship, I told myself. Would Mandy know Rodney?

The drudgery of the school day passed, and I was thinking of tonight's party with Uncle and his daughter. The approaching sound of the footsteps brought me to my senses, and I realized Mandy was just point-blank staring at me: "Anky, you alright? "She whispered. "Yes, yes, I was just thinking about tonight's party with Uncle. " . Come to think about it, I was also wondering about tonight's party. And which dress should I wear, Anky? "Would the red dress go well?" "Mandy" you are gorgeous, any dress will go with you, and you know you are my sister: I always speak the truth, saying that we both laughed. She went to change her dress, I too went into my room and started searching for the "best dress to wear" and I chose a light blue full sleeves shirt with dark matching trousers. I looked into the mirror, poked out my tongue at the reflection, and returned a gentle smile at my reflection. I heard Mandy speaking to someone on the phone: Yes, we are ready and leaving in just 5 minutes. "You ready, Anky, let us go "Mandy shouted from the doorway. I am ready and stepped out of my room. Mandy rushed to her room and grabbed the pair of gloves, my gift packet, and we splashed out of the house. "Anky", what is the matter? why are you so excited? In fact, you are excited and why are you carrying these gloves? "I want uncle to see these pretty gloves, and she waved out at my face. "Okay, Mandy, let us go out now, the time is up.

Chapter 4

Disco-Like Trendy Hotel

We called a passing cab and told the driver to take us to Hotel Marriot at Bandstand, Bandra. The driver told us to get in and he turned the meter on. In approximately twenty minutes' drive we reached Band Stand, Bandra: HOTEL MARRIOT. It was an elite suburb of Mumbai, where the neo rich people (like Uncle Jerry) and Bollywood stars lived. Hence, there was a lot of security staff and police personnel moving about.

We had to cross the street at the signals as the hotel was on the opposite side of the road. In the blinking lights, we walked hand in hand and reached Marriot, where the security guard let us in with a warm welcome smile. We walked through the corridor, and turned right, and we could see the Disco lights neon board "WONGKIN" --- our today's venue. The attendant at the entrance asked us our names and booking references. Upon hearing our names, the attendant told us our table no. was 29 P, on the right side of the entrance door. We thanked him and entered the dinning-hall looking for table No 29 P. A female staff accompanied us to the "P" area. (we did not know what the 29 P meant, but later understood from Uncle Jerry that it was "Prestigious seating arrangements ") We saw, Uncle Jerry and Sherry were already seated, and they got up from their seats and welcomed us with chants of "Good Evening, Good Evening "We settled down in the well illuminated hall with twinkling lights in the roof. There was a light orchestra playing in the far end of the room. There was a modest crowd of trendy youngsters in and around. The waiters brought us some welcome soft drinks and left us to enjoy our company.

Uncle Jerry gave his approval for ordering whatever we liked and sharing it together. Uncle saw the package in Mandy's hands and politely inquired what it was. When Mandira told him it was a birthday gift from Anky, a pair of boxing gloves, Sherry's eyes gleamed "I too want it. You look so macho wearing beautiful gloves. We all laughed, and Mandy wore it on her hands and punched a blow in the air! Then

Sherry kissed the gloves and rubbed her hand all over it, bracing her hands on the soft leather, like she was petting a cat! Uncle Jerry laughed. Much impressed with a newer kind of a Birthday gift! I promised Sherry that I would get her a pair of the same gloves on her birthday! "No, no, you don't, I shall ask my dad to get one similar pair for me" replied Sherry. Uncle Jerry promised his daughter to get one pair in the next week: provided she uses, else it will become a show piece in her collection. Sherry made a face and said to Mandy "I am sure my sister will train me for some boxing stunts, as I do fear boys on the street--- she said laughingly to Mandira. "No problem, you are welcome for a "macho" season once you decide to take a keen interest in boxing, or Judo, or Karate, as I am well trained in defensive arts and have won several trophies, Mandira replied to Sherry. With peace regained, we accepted our soft drinks from the bartender who just delivered us our drinks, queerly looking at Mandira wearing gloves! But he slightly moved away his eyes from her to face us with a smile saying ,"Enjoy your drinks", as he left, he still took a backward glance eyeing Mandira's gloves.

Another waiter approached us and asked if we were ready to order. Uncle Jerry requested us to select our dishes from the menu and place orders. For starters, Mandy wanted tomato soup, Sherry craved sweet corn soup, Uncle said he preferred broccoli soup, and I settled for spinach soup. The waiter took down the soup list and said it would at least take 15 minutes for preparation, and in the meantime, we could decide on the main course. Saying that, he disappeared towards the kitchen area.

A group of youngers passed by our table, among them a tall fellow looked at Mandira, commenting "look a lady-in-red with boxing gloves" and broke into mocking laughter. Mandira gave him a piercing glance while we silently observed the scene. Nothing untoward happened and we sipped our drinks. After a few minutes, Sherry said she wanted to use the washroom and asked Mandira to accompany her. Both the girls left, and Uncle Jerry asked me the address of the shop from where I got the gloves. I told him, just near my school is the "Maxwell Sports Studio and I paid IRS Sixteen hundred for the gloves. Uncle exclaimed "A good deal young man, nice thoughtful gift for your sister, as she is always up to something new in the sports field," "Yes, you said it Uncle. Mandy is always practicing boxing, judo, karate and what not…. You should look at the collection of sports prizes she has won: Always on top --- never a runner up. We heard a commotion some meters away from our table, and sensing some trouble, we rushed towards the noisy area, wishing it was not our girls in the chaos. Sure enough, our Mandira was standing there, with her right hand firmly clasped on the neck of a tall fellow, yelling, next time you tease us, you will get a real thrashing, pushing the tall guy with a hard force sending him limping backwards. His two other colleagues were folding their hands and requesting Mandira to let it go…. He won't tease her next time. Uncle ventured forward and held the arm of Mandira requesting her to let go and join us at the table. The tall guy got up dusting his pants, and saying "Sorry, Sorry, I did not mean to be eve-teasing, just let me go and I apologize for my conduct. Saying thus, all three boys left towards the exit and moved out of the hotel immediately, not turning back once to see us or the approaching barman. The barman came to us, offered his apologies, and said the security guards will deal with the offenders, as the alarm bell was on. Meantime, he requested us to go back to our seats and calm down. Assured in a meaningful way, we turned towards our table, when Mandy told us, "The guy was calling me ...Red, Red, Red... and I lost my temper, gave him a hard punch on his cheek and caught his neck almost strangling him... he could not breathe for a moment and I released my grip, yet held up my arm swaying in the air. His colleagues faltered and started apologizing, realizing I was too strong for all of them. Yet, a short statured guy came charging at me with his two closed fists. Impulsively, I flung my right leg sideways, towards his charge, and he was thrown away like a fly. He was unable to get up and a passerby helped him get up, thrashing him further with a slap, shouting "You don't have any shame in attacking a lady, did your parents not teach you any manners". Instinctively, I calmed down, realizing the situation was now under control. The boys' rough noise brought the crowd to this area: I saw a security officer dressed in white dress with a pen and pad in his hand. I told him we (pointing to Sherry) had just come out of the washroom when the tall rowdy guy called out "Red Red "pointing at my dress. The security officer calmed me down and said he had watched the bunch of rowdy boys on the secret camera and was following them and witnessed the brief fight. Security personnel apologized to me and had called his bouncers to take care of the situation.

The bouncers had cornered the ruffians and driven them out of the hotel. That is when Uncle and Anky came here.

Back on our seats, people seemed to applaud Mandy for her bravery and looked at us cheerfully. Mandy apologized for her stint but assured us she did it for self-respect and protection of herself and Sherry, least something untoward could have happened in the washroom area. Mandy composed herself and requested all of us to ignore the incident and not to mention anyone, including her parents, in Kuwait. We assured and reassured her, as she did not want any scene, but it was just an unfortunate incident. Sherry had the audacity to ask for self-defense training course! making all of us laugh! "Uncle, did I do anything wrong? "Mandy queried. "Not at all, Not, at all, in fact, I think you did a wise thing, as even my daughter was along with you: she is too timid and would have got scared very easily and cried. Thanks for being with her, I appreciate your stand."

There was a sigh of relief on Mandy's face, and she seemed to be more relaxed now. "Come to think of it, I was asking Mandira to train me in sports" quipped in Sherry. And they both laughed. Mandy made a sensible statement: "Listen, I am practicing Yoga, Boxing, Judo, Karate, et al not for defense purposes, but for my physical fitness. Remember, when we were children, we could put our toenail in our mouth effortlessly. Now, tell me how many of us can do that sort of a thing? "You see", she continued "our body is quite capable of keeping us healthy and lively, provided we feed nourishing food and good thoughts…. yes. Constant words in our mind become our thoughts, I believe. Our Lord has made us perfect in every way, but that does not mean we abuse our bodies by neglecting it. If we choose good food, healthy habits, meditate, live harmoniously with Nature I am sure all can live well without getting sick or diseased. I firmly believe Yoga helps me in breathing and mediation, Judo, Karate, etc., etc., help you in making your body tough and strong muscles--- enough to guarantee good health throughout our life. There was a round of clap from Uncle, Sherry and me--- all the tables across us glanced at us and waved –for whatever reasons. *"Uncle, longevity, without good health is a curse"* Mandy ended.

There came a pause in our talks and rightly, the waiter brought us steaming hot food oozing with aroma of freshness and various spices! Each of us took a little helping from all dishes. By the look of it, the food was enough for all four of us, and we did not want to have leftovers as carry- home packs! This is a dictum we always maintained. A few minutes later, a waiter came to check on us: Was the food good? Would we be ordering anything more? Would we care to have some desserts? Our answer to everything was a firm "No". Then the waiter added "May I ask who is Mandira? We have a Birthday Treat for Mandira: A Chocolate Ice-cream on a Dark Sizzling Brownie! All of us smiled brightly forgetting the recent bad episode. The waiter continued: It is a gift from our F & B department. The idea was conveyed to us by Jerry Simon while booking this table, last week. We all looked up to Uncle Jerry and uttered: Thank You Uncle Jerry for such a wonderful surprise treat", Thank You, Thank You So Very Much and we all went in a circle with a dance step around the table. We clapped, the onlookers clapped, and the waiter gave an order for his crew to bring the coveted surprise dish! The dish was eloquently done with a lavish spread of red cherries and chocolates. It was a real mouth-watering surprise, and we once again thanked Uncle Jerry for his kindness. The feast was soon over, and we all enjoyed the beautiful sweet-dish complimenting the Baker's artistic presentation.

Uncle told us his car was in the hotel's parking lot and he would drop us home whenever we wished to. Since the next day, was a Sunday, we were quite relaxed and enjoyed family talks. It was customary for guests to wave out to diners and we enjoyed the friendly atmosphere. It was getting past eleven and we decided to call it quits: Uncle promised we shall meet again during Christmas time when our parents would be here on holidays.

We all decided to go to a new venture when our parents came --- all agreed, and we left the premises happily. On the way out, the F&B manager, SAM WILMORE, greeted us, giving us his visiting card, saying we could come here once again and earn a loyalty discount of 15% on Food and Beverages. We thanked him and wished him Good Night but did not accept his visiting card.

Chapter 5

The Mysterious Call

Getting up on a Sunday morning was a pleasure. It meant opening my eyes, yet dreamy, and not having any urgency to jump out of bed. I loved to wake up lazily, particularly on a Sunday, or rather on any other holiday. This was unlike Mandy, who was always up at the same time--- be it a working day or a holiday. She hated to get up by an alarm clock and prided herself as a "Sun Riser". True, the slight noise emerging from the kitchen confirmed she had finished her exercises and was up to making something as "Sunday Special "Yes, that also meant she would be having two cups of tea instead of the usual one cup in the morning. "Are you awake, Anky, I can't hear any snoring — that was her usual tease-pull on me. And I would pretend to snore heavily, but she was too clever to know that I was faking. She would again call "Tea is 50% cold by now, do you want an ice cream tea?"

All along, I knew she wanted me to come down and talk with her and she had made no tea for me --- just pulling my leg to make me leave the bed and talk to her. Taking her cue, I crept out of the warm bed and turned to the washroom. The water was cold to the touch, and I enjoyed the dip. Within 20 minutes I was out of the washroom and slowly crept into the kitchen and whispered in Mandy's ear: Where is the ice cream T? And she put an ice-cold white onion in my hand. "Aah" I shrieked --- a white onion? "Does it not look like Vanilla Ice cream ball? Mandy replied with a mischievous twinkle in her eye. "Tea is on the kettle, will be served shortly" and Mandy disappeared around the kitchen shelf to bring out my teacup. "Mandy, what did you dream yesterday? Had a good sleep? "Thanks, I had a wonderful sleep," she replied, pouring tea in my cup. "And how about you, Anky? Did you sleep well? Mandy asked me. "Yes, oh! Yes, was tired from the late-night outing, touched the pillow and went to sleep. Thank you" I replied. Well, Anky, what will you like for breakfast? "Mandy, I shall make my own breakfast ---fastest in the world --- cornflakes!! She gleamed and I added: do you want me to make for you also, as it is the simplest breakfast anyone can ever make! "No, if you can, make me an egg omelet with pieces of tomatoes, onions, cheese, coriander leaves and salt n pepper" Mandy replied with a twinkle in her eye--- meaning she did not want an "easy breakfast" like cornflakes!! Goody, Good, Good, we liked to tease each other!

The phone rang and I hurried to pick. Usually on Sundays, Mom and Dad speak to us from Kuwait. But the voice at the other end was a new --- a female voice asking for Mandira. "Mandy, this call is for you, I called Mandy holding the mouthpiece. Please come and take the call. "Hello, this is Mandira, who is this please? my sister queried on the phone. "I am Cathy Vaz, a classmate of the same school where your brother, Ankesh goes to. "Yes, that is right but what do you want from me? Mandy replied with a little irritation. "I understand you are good at sports; I would like to get private lessons from you, I am 12 years old and just live across your place: 31, Pali Hill. Rodney is my brother, and he too goes to K Club but I need a private tutor hence I called you. "OK, Cathy, listen, we are strangers till now, if we could meet each other sometimes in K Club area, then later I could tell you more on subject you are interested in. "Thank you so much, Madame Mandira, your brother, Anky, is a very sweet boy: I met him in the school bus, and he is very shy, and if he is around, could I tell him "Hi", if he is not around, just give him my regards, and she hung up. Mandira called me and asked about this this girl Cathy and the present conversation. I was shy to talk about Cathy and more so about this talk held early in the morning hours. I wanted my parents to call and later in the daytime we could talk about this new acquaintance. Mandy nodded her head in agreement, and we set on our fixed duties for this Sunday morning: washing clothes, ironing, house cleaning, lunch preparation, et all with a clock work precision. Yet, we both were upset as our parents had still not called us.

I said I will do my washing of clothes first, then ironing the earlier lot, also then ironing my sister's clothes. Then I would do shoe-polishing and dusting and sweeping of the floor. Later we both would go to the market for the weekly groceries. Mandy approved the household home assignments and said she would decide about lunch and dinner in the later part of the day. Luckily, the telephone rang, and this time Mandy grabbed the phone and confidently said "Hi Mom".... She moved away the earpiece and was yelling "Who is this online now, and why do you want to know my details....? After a little pause she uttered

"OK, well then come now and take my signature on your courier paper" and she banged the phone on the cradle. I was a bit shocked and afraid---I calmly called "Mandy, who was this caller now? "That stupid courier man, he said while I got the draft, I did not sign the acknowledgement copy the other day and is coming to take my signature within 20 minutes! I am getting worried why our parents have not called us so far, usually they call us by 9 am... and now it is 10am already. Mandy said "Anky, do you think we should call them now or wait for some more time? "I replied, wait for some fifteen minutes, then we shall call. There was a ring on the doorbell and the courier man had come --- I saw him from the peep hole. Mandy headed towards the door and at the same time the phone also rang. I picked up the call but did not say a word: maybe it could be someone else and not our parents' call – did not want any surprises anymore. "Ankesh Baba, Good morning, how are you? And I could hear my mom's loving voice: Everything alright? My pets, where is Mandira? "Mom, we are both fine but were just wondering why your call did not come --- usually you call us by 9am... everything alright mom? I queried. "Yes, yes, all is fine, dad is here too, put the speaker on we want to hear both of you. Mandy hurried and quickly joined me "Mummy

/ Daddy, we are missing you, how we wish we were all together now and Mandy started sobbing". "Sweetie, Sweetie," my dad's voice echoed please don't cry only two more months and we shall come down for Christmas with lots of gifts for both of you. I held Mandy's hand and kissed her hand "Mandy please don't cry, if you don't stop, even I will cry, and I swallowed my words, now petting her hair. Daddy whistled a tune, and it brought us memories how we were eager to hear his tune when we were young. Hearing the tune, Mandy composed, petted my head and become normal. "Yes, dad, we are counting the days, two months are 60 days, and we are yearning to see you here. Mom said, "how are your studies going on, Anky? And how are your Judo and Karate sessions going on, Mandira? I popped in "Mom, Mandy is learning boxing too, and I gave her a pair of Boxing gloves as her birthday gift. "Yes, mama and dad, Anky gave me a beautiful pair of gloves—I LOVE IT. "Oh, we are so happy "And how did your birthday go? Where did you go to celebrate? "Mum, your cousin, --Uncle Jerry took us to Marriot Hotel near Pali Hill. You remember, you took us there on your last trip here? His daughter Sherry was also there --- we had a good dinner along with a complimentary dessert from their F&B division... it was wonderful:

wish you were there too! Uncle Jerry also dropped us way back…. We truly enjoyed it. "Good Mandy, you told us, we shall call Jerry and speak to him after this call," mom replied. "And Mom/ Dad, thank you for the wonderful gift you sent us …. The courier forgot to take my signature on the delivery note and has just come now to collect my signature. Thanks A Lot, once again, mom and dad. "Mum, when you come from Kuwait, please get me some Kuwaiti coins and stamps, as I love to collect, I replied to my mum. "Okay, Cheers, now, we are going to the church now, mom and dad replied simultaneously." OK, BYE, see you soon, and they hung up the line. We both had tears in our eyes—loneliness is an unkind gift.

I dried my eyes with tissue paper and wiped tears from Mandy's cheeks. We consoled each other, yet happy, our parents would soon return to Mumbai. Mandy gave a good suggestion: we shall call Uncle Jerry and Sherry in the evening and convey our parents' regards.

Mandy left towards the laundry area, peeped behind the door and satisfied, there were not many clothes to wash and iron. Satisfied, she turned towards me and said "Anky, if the workload is too much for you, please call me and I shall help you out. Now I am going to change the bed sheets, pillowcases, clean all the rooms with the vacuum cleaner, etc. In case you need anything do let me know. I hope you had something for breakfast: there were cheese croissants, soft buns, biscuits and chips. "No worries, I had some bites here and there, and I am OK. Hope, Mandy, you too had something for breakfast. "Yes", and she went towards my bedroom.

Peacefully we did our weekly jobs without any fuss and were happy to notice that about two hours had passed and all the jobs were attended to. We met in the saloon and sat down on the sofa for some rest and light soft drinks. I had stretched myself on the sofa, while Mandy had seated herself on the chair next to me. I could feel her long hair touching my arms and I was enjoying the little tickling sensation on my right arm. Realizing this, she rubbed my head with her soft hand, and it reminded me of my mom doing so when I was a little boy of four or five years old. I was feeling sleepy, and Mandy, noticing this, told me to order a takeaway from "Food Bites" a nice restaurant nearby our house. We both were happy with this decision as we both were foodies ---on a weekend! Mandy had a part time job besides her college studies. Yesterday she had got her salary, and she had decided to give me a treat—afternoon lunch and an evening treat too! I knew she was very fond of me, and I had decided to open the topic of Cathy Vaz and her brother, Rodney. She disappeared into the kitchen to make lemon juice for me and herself, as she was very conscious of her health regime. There was a knock on the door, and the delivery boy had brought our lunch. Mandy advised to have lunch after thirty minutes of drinking the lime juice. This was a good pause time for me to bring out the topic of Cathy Vaz. "Mandy, do you know anyone as "Rodney" who is also a member of K Club – the place where you go to for your work outs? Cathy Vaz is his sister, who is my school mate, and I meet her in the school bus". Mandy replied, with a shy glance: who is Cathy Vaz... the one who gave us a call in the morning? And she told me you are very shy...Mandy added. "True "I said. Yesterday, Cathy sat next to me in the bus and told me your sister is extremely good in Judo/Karate/Boxing, et all and her brother, Rodney, said so. Hence, she asked to train under your guidance. As we had no commitments in the evening, I suggest we go to Pali Compound and tell them to join us there. "Good idea, Anky, let us do that "But you call Cathy and confirm if it is OK with them. Also, this reminds me, after lunch, we shall call Uncle Jerry and speak to him and Sherry. "Oh! I had forgotten about them, good, after lunch we shall speak to them and after that I shall call Cathy. "Sounds good" Mandy replied, and, in a few moments, we settled for lunch. Mandy took a larger portion of salad items and conversely, I took a larger portion of French fries! Taste matters for foodies! We finished our lunch in a very relaxed way, Mandy telling me about her part time job matters and how she rarely talks with men in the office, though there are more men than women in the workplace. The boss is very kind and is liberal about working hours, as he knows I am a college student. Just then, the phone rang, and it was Uncle Jerry online. "Long life, Uncle Jerry, we were just thinking to call you today in the evening, Mandy said, keeping the phone on open volume. We could hear Uncle Jerry laughing and the voice of Sherry in the background. "Well, our parents have sent you warm regards and thank you very much for the treat bestowed on us. We all spoke on conference line and each person had a fair share of family talks, much to the satisfaction of everybody. The call lasted for about 20 minutes.

Later I called Cathy, who was delighted to hear my voice, and had just returned from church. Upon my asking for a meeting point, she quickly agreed, for a meeting point at the K Club Garden area at 6pm. She would come with Rodney, her elder brother. She asked me to bring Mandira along. "Yes" I replied, and we went for a small afternoon nap in our respective rooms.

Mandira was in two minds: Was her practicing of tough sports like boxing, judo, karate, and soft activities like Yoga and Meditation in tune with her current circle of friends? Her friend Jemima was also in such activities, except Jemima did not practice Yoga. Yasin, her college mate, was only into Yoga and had a very slender body. She was a walking beauty and was running a friendly Free Yoga class on her building terrace in the early morning hours. Yet, another friend of hers, Amina, was into karate learning, and holding a Black Belt at the age of seventeen years! Now, the question in her mind arose: why did Cathy want to learn Karate from her. She had said her brother was a member of K Club, and K Club taught many sports, including Karate. Was it because she knew my brother, Anky, was her classmate and, perhaps Anky had told her so? One thing was sure: Mandira was quite athletic and loved these sports for her own sake: she was very health conscious and rarely felt ill. That is one reason she was so disciplined in life and very particular about food and healthy habits, Perhaps, she was a copy of our father --- tall, muscular and handsome --- yet a poor eater by every count: just like herself.

Sitting alone in my room, I was feeling a bit uneasy. I needed the company of my sister, Mandy. For some odd reasons, the face of Cathy Vaz came to mind. Why did she want to meet me and Mandy and learn Judo or Karate from her? Ladies are complex creatures, I could not understand – for instance, why did Mandy cry when our parents called us in the morning. I have also seen Mandy as a tough person, a righteous person and I was astonished at her wailing in the morning hours. It was a joy to talk to mama and papa, and suddenly, she become emotional and cried--- which also dragged some tears in my eyes: it was a reflex action. Back to my thoughts: why did Cathy touch my arm with a smile? And then, why she did not talk to me on the phone in the morning? She spoke to Mandy, even without knowing her. And who told her Mandy has an expert in Karate / Judo / etc. Yes, she did say her brother mentioned her name, as he must have known some K club members. Anyway, I had questions to ask Cathy when we would meet. The alarm clock chimed four pm and I thought I must take rest for an hour or so to refresh myself. Soon I dozed off.

Chapter 6

The Meeting

Mandy brought a cup of tea in my room saying "Be quick, drink this tea, and when you are ready, we set out to Pali Hill, K Club area. "Yes, I remember, got some sleep, don't know how…. shall be ready in fifteen minutes. Meanwhile, Mandy combed her hair, looking in the circular mirror hung up on the wall. She took some tissues and wiped the mirror, shaking the mirror a little. After adjusting the mirror, she drew out a pencil liner and neatly rubbed over her eyebrows, darkening the eyebrow hair line. With a mischievous grin, she came forward to me and asked "Do you too want your eyebrows darkened, my pet? I laughed and tilted my neck back. This is what I liked about my sister, she would make funny statements and take me for a ride! On an impulse, I took some water in my hand and asked her "do you want me to splash the water and clean the mirror?" "Yes, Yes, please

do that, I shall have a greater shine in my reflection"
I laughed and splashed a handful of water and
gently wiped the mirror--- yes it became foggy for
a moment and then cleared away the mist. Mandy
peeped sideways in the mirror and satisfied, sat on
the chair and told me to get dressed up, meanwhile
she too will change and get ready. In another ten
minutes, we shall be leaving--- and tomorrow is
a working day, should get back home as early as
possible.

We came hand in hand to K club area and found
an empty bench, a little away from the main entrance
of K Club. From this vantage point, we could see the
people enter and exit. This was a comfortable seat,
and we reserved the full bench for us --- by keeping
Mandy's handbag and my hat in between us. As
many people kept going in and out of the entrance,
I had to tilt my face every now and then to monitor
the arrival of Cathy and her brother. Cathy had
described her brother as a tall guy, so it was easy
for me to test check the arrivals of my classmate,
Cathy. No such luck for about fifteen minutes, till I
saw Cathy arriving alone and occasionally throwing
a glance every which way she could trace me and
Mandy. I got up and called out "Cathy, Cathy, we

are here and waved my hand too. On the contrary, she now looked the other way and was wondering if someone had called her. Then I told Mandy, you sit here on the bench and mind things, I shall run across to her and bring her here. "Alright, Mandy said, and I ran towards Cathy, yet another time calling her name a bit loudly, so she could hear. "Hi! Hi! She turned around and noticed me and came walking towards me. I was glad I had finally spotted her, but where was her brother?

Cathy caught hold of my hand, though I felt a bit shy, but she seemed to be unmoved and asked where is Mandira? "Over there, on the bench, a little further down: we have occupied the full wooden bench, least someone comes and sits on and then our privacy will be gone". Clever of you, and she pecked my cheek lightly with a kiss. I was embarrassed yet not wanting to be annoyed, I asked her where her brother was or, did she come alone? We were soon reaching Mandy, and she ran into a short run and held her two arms wide in the air and embraced affectionately my sister. It was a hearty hug and even Mandy was surprised with her warmth. Mandy shook Cathy's arm and gave her a warm hug too. Cathy appeared tiny in front of Mandira, as my sister was well built and quite tall. After the pleasantries were over, Mandy said: Well, I suppose you were supposed to come with your brother, weren't you? "Oh Yes, I was supposed to come with Roland, but at the last moment his friend called him for a movie and reluctantly he told me to go alone, at least you two would be offended. "Offended we are, as we expected to meet your brother too, but it is a disappointment, you could have informed us earlier and we could have rescheduled the meeting some other time. "Never mind, we shall go the club café and have some tea inside, Is that OK with you, Cathy?" Mandy coolly whispered. "Sounds good" Cathy replied, and we proceeded to the entrance of K Club. *There was an uneasy feeling between all three of us, I somehow felt.*

Luckily, Cathy caught Mandy's left hand, and I walked on the right side of Mandy without catching her hand. We took slow steps moving between the crowded lane, all heading to the main entrance of the club. Only Mandy had the membership card to the K Club and the security asked for the cards of Cathy and me. Since we did not have the cards, the security guard asked us to go to the cashier and pay the entrance fees or else we could not go in with

Mandy. It was a bad decision and Mandy reasoned, it would be better to go out and have tea somewhere else, rather than pay the hefty Club admission fees. We all nodded and soon made a U turn towards the "K's WAYSIDE CAFETERIA" a few meters away from the entrance of K Club. That settled our restlessness, and we cheered for INSTA COFFEE – a sort of Creamy White Milk Coffee, which we all loved.

"And now, tell me, Cathy, what is your interest in going for Karate classes with me? Mandy inquired of Cathy. Cathy was silent for a moment, then she said "just for the heck of it" I want to learn Karate. Then she took a pause before replying "I am always frightened to go out alone and am always afraid of boys attacking me. To counterattack my mental fright, I would like to practice karate. "Cathy, I am afraid both of your reasonings are wrong according to me", Mandy replied in a dignified way. First, you do not learn a sport with an ulterior reason, and second, even if you were to learn an art, your mis concept about "afraid of the boys" does not go well with it. The fear you have is an internal concern, not a logical concern, I feel" Mandy concluded her statement. I was astonished by my sister's insight of things, and mentally applauded her. My sister took a sip of coffee waiting for a further reply from Cathy. Cathy's eyes were moist, and she softly said "Okay, Mandy, please tell me how best I can learn Karate as I have a gut feeling I need to learn for self-defense or even for my pleasure. Anyway, please tell me something about karate training under you. "My simple advice to you is to read some write up on karate training for beginners. It would be helpful to you to know about steps to go about, till you finally get a Black Belt, if that is your desire. For one thing, know it, it is a tough sport, your body must be firm yet flexible, get used to tough chops from the opponent, learn physiological elements, of how body energy is conserved and expended. This is all in the theory and practical classes of karate, I hope you understand, Mandy concluded. Yet, a piece of advice I would like to give you is: Do pull-ups. Do rigorous pull ups --- in a few months you will notice you have gained inches in height. Yes, that should be your aim, I am suggesting pull ups as I feel you are short, and the best way is to do pull ups as you are very young and quite adaptable to changes in body. "Thanks, Mandira from today itself, I shall catch up with pull-up exercises.

I finished my coffee sip by sip listening to the expertise of my sister, who had also just finished her coffee. There was a long pause before my sister asked Cathy: who told you, I am good at Karate and could also teach you karate? Cathy took a deep breath and replied: I often come to K Club with my brother for observing and passing time in the club: My brother told the club management my sister is interested in sports and would like to join the club later, in the meantime, could they let me in the club just to watch the club activities. They agreed only for one month, provided I came with my brother only, and not alone. In the time I have been coming to the club, I have heard many members talk highly about you: and always point out to whenever you pass by. So, I am determined to be like you, even my brother Roland, once commented, there is a lady by name, "Mandira" who rules the roost here in Judo/Karate/Boxing/etc. classes. That is how I gathered information from the club members ---- and you became my distant mentor. That is the truth --- my brother said he had not seen you but heard much about you from the club members. That is why, I told Ankesh, I need to meet you. We were all silent for some time.

Shall we leave now? I asked Cathy. Yes, we can leave, shall ask my brother, Roland, to make a next meeting and surely, we shall meet all together, I promise. When we got up, Cathy said "Thank You for the coffee, lovely meeting, shall soon meet once again. Looking at Mandy, she continued "Mandira, your height is just like Roland's: he is also tall like you, and she giggled. "Take Care, Cathy", don't be afraid of boys, I am sure I will not attack you anytime, I said cheerfully. She laughed, and held my hand, saying "You are such a silent bird, you won't harm an insect" and she placed her other hand in the palms of Mandira, saying "Ankesh is a sweet shy boy". Mandira laughed and mischievously added "Yes, Cathy, and he likes you" I turned pale, and Cathy, said "even the teachers call him a SHY BOY". I did not know whether I should laugh or cry... the only words that came from my mouth was "Goodnight". I held my both hands with Mandy's hands and just uttered "Bye". But Cathy came forward, touched my face with her right hand and said Bye, Shy Boy". I oozed a smile at her and she winked!

Onwards, towards our home, Mandira made a comment: let us have a sandwich or a burger with tea, as I am a bit dazed with today's absurd meeting. Even I had felt the same thing when we were sitting on the bench: *An uneasy feeling.*

We stopped at the "Baker's Delight" café at the junction of Pali Hill and Bandra Signals—just a few minutes away from our house. We ordered a strong cup of tea along with an egg burger and a vegetable sandwich. In the shadowy night we saw Cathy walking along with a tall guy. From our higher seats, we could see their backs, and guessed the tall boy was Roland, her brother. Was this a chance meeting with her brother? Or had she phoned him to pick her up since she was afraid of walking alone, and that too at night--- it was nearing 7pm now. Good they did not see us, but we saw them. Mandy got up from her seat and peeped hard from the windowpane: she wanted to see a closeup of Roland but could not get a better view as Roland and Cathy were moving away and their frame was diminishing. For some odd reasons I believed it was Roland who had teased me "Red, Red" in the hotel, the other day, and I had bashed him up! I told my thoughts to Anky, who did not comment on anything at first. After some time, he asked me: it could be our imagination only. Did we see Roland's face? "No" we both replied at the same time. Then, why go far in thinking? That set right our mood, and we continued enjoying our snacks.

Chapter 7

The First Day of the Week

It was Monday morning, the beginning of the new week, and the last week of the month. Good, after seven days, Dad will send us the monthly expenses allowances for household expenses. I would need Mandy's quick calculations of the outflows and mentally guess the approximate savings we could make this month. Each month, on an average, we happened to save Rupees Five Thousand Indian Rupees. So, by year end we should have at least Fifty Thousand ---enough to buy a Christmas Gift for our parents! Though they would not like us to spend money on them, we still had the pleasure of saving and buying a gift for our dear parents. Anyway, who does not like a Gift? And that too during Christmas? My thoughts were running helter-skelter with joyous feeling --- our biggest gifts would not be the gifts our parents would be bringing from Kuwait, but their very presence in the house would be much more rewarding than anything else! Twenty-two months is a long wait! That is what our parents' contract was --- twenty-two months of work and 2 months of vacation!

It was only when the clock struck 7 in the morning, I realized I was late in completing my morning chores! I gave my breakfast pack to Mandy, who was delighted to have it as she was getting late for the office! I pecked her forehead and she in turn rolled my hair on her arm drawing me closer to herself. After a little tug-o-war, she gently let off go my entangled hair--- much to my delight. Our mornings were always splashed with little gimmicks before we departed outside our house ---she for her college and office and me for school. We both had finished our morning chores and were ready to leave.

Mandy left saying "BYE" and I collected the house key and soon left as I sensed the school bus was coming. The school bus was waiting on the hazard, and I quickly crossed the road and got onto the bus. I saw a waving hand and noticed Cathy was calling me to sit next to her, but because an empty seat was just near the entrance of the bus, I plunged myself there due to the bus in motion. I turned around and looked back at Cathy and just waved my hand. She was satisfied and waved her hand.

Getting off the bus, I waited for Cathy to climb down the bus and walk along with her to our classroom. We exchanged "Good mornings" and the first question I asked was how she went home yesterday after our meeting in the K Club. Well, she said she was afraid to go alone, and since her brother was in the next building in the theatre, she phoned him and he told her to wait outside the cinema hall and he would meet her in ten minutes time. This explanation put me at ease as she had already told me her brother had gone for a movie with his friend. Good, I could relate this to Mandy in the evening. At our respective classrooms, we separated.

Arithmetic is my favorite subject but not my Arithmetic teacher. Mr. Sam Timothy always gives us tough questions to solve and expects all students to pass in his class. His theory was: If you fail, it means I have failed. In my mind, I would have loved to share my answers with weaker students--- but he would not allow it. So, I had devised a way out --- during lunch break, I would voluntarily teach the students who were weak in math's. Two students, Harry and Daniel approached me to sit next to them so they could better understand the subject and copy from my book, if need be. This was a hush-hush arrangement, and likewise, even some other students who were strong in arithmetic would try to help classmates. We were quite social with all classmates, except some toughies who made fists at us! This was the scene, I guessed prevailing in other classes too.

Sam Timothy entered the class whispering something, perhaps to himself. "Good morning, Sir" we echoed, and he responded Good Morning, Good Morning, Good Morning. "OK", how many times, I repeated "Good Morning" said Sam Timothy, trying to enlighten us before his tough session could get started. "Three Times, we responded. "Well, if you pay attention to my subject, I shall repeat each explanation three times, like I repeated "Good Morning" and be sure to pay attention. If someone does not follow me, raise your hand, and I shall repeat once again. I don't want any student to fail in math's --- in fact, I believe, math's is the easiest subject to learn, if you pay 100% attention. We nodded and kept silent to grasp his explanation. Fortunately, all went well, except two students who got the answers right after the second attempt. We waited for our next class: Geography, the interesting one! Time passed quickly, and History and Science class too passed, and the bell struck one o'clock for our short break.

I was having my sandwich, when I noticed Cathy was waving at me from a distance. She came forward and said this coming weekend we shall meet, as her brother messaged her to inform you. I said, the weekend is still far, and we shall decide by Friday. "Ok" she said and rushed to her class. My classmate Gilbert asked me to share his snacks with him as he did not bring any food for himself since he got up late. We shared and happily discussed class events. Gilbert informed me he too stays near K Club, and he had seen me with Cathy and "one tall lady" last weekend. I explained to Gilbert that "tall lady" is my sister Mandira. He said "I guessed so, I wanted to join you but was somehow shy and did not come to the bench where you all were sitting. You know, I stay in the same building, where Cathy stays. She is on top floor; I am on the first floor. "Ankesh, I have heard your sister is good in sports like Karate, Judo, Boxing, etc. Does she give private classes --- I would be very interested as we have a large balcony, and I could also tell my friends to join us, if she does not mind.

It will be a win-win situation for all of us! I have seen your sister from far and am bowled by her figure – she looks exactly like a Fitness Trainer. Think about it and let me know please. Anyway, some other time, whenever you come to that area, just give me a buzz and we can meet in my house. "Alright, good idea shall keep in mind," I replied to Gilbert. "Does Cathy have a brother, named Rodney?" Gilbert successfully threw the five fingers of his right hand opening and closing in the air. I got the whiff of it: "useless, good for nothing". I added one more information to relate to Mandy.

The bell rang and we moved to our respective classrooms for the second part of the day. For some reason, some students, including me, yawned in the classroom, much to the disgust of Joline Periera, our Geography teacher. "Ankesh, I know you are clever in the class and geography is one of your favorite subjects, still, why are you yawning in the class" Shamefully, I apologized "Sorry, Teacher. Other students who had also yawned, kept their faces down--- one victim is a lesson in the classroom.

As we caught the school bus returning us back to our homes, I noticed Cathy's face was small. Looks like she had a bad day at school. "Everything alright? I asked. She did not reply but turned away her face. Meera, her friend replied to me "Cathy did not do well in her arithmetic test: The teacher scolded her, and she has felt bad. "No" that is NOT the reason, Cathy replied sharply. But I shall not tell anything to anyone. "Mind your business, Meera" and Cathy looked downwards. At the other end of the bus, there was a small fight: Daryll wanted to sit near the window and Kenny was not allowing him to occupy that seat, as he had climbed the bus earlier! I was unnerved by the routine drama on the school bus. Even the conductor, John, was helpless as he too could not manage about thirty students: some tall, some short, some fat, some skinny, and still some girls elegant, but better behaved than boys. My destination came and I got down, waving a "Bye" to Cathy, who was composed by now.

Giving myself a face wash and changing my dress, I rushed to the fridge to see if there is a lemonade or a Juice to still my nerves. I was also guilty of yawning in the class and upset about Cathy who did not respond properly to me. Also, the talk with Gilbert and his indiscriminate reply about Rodney. The fight for the window seat between Kenny and the other classmate

--- I forgot his name. The lemonade refreshed me, and I said to myself: why am I thinking about all the day's wear outs? Enough. I got up and put on the TV to see the news, rather than watch the funny cartoons appearing in the middle of advertisements! I loved the cartoons Tom and Jerry, among the best of best cartoons! Sometimes I thought Mandy and I were also like Tom and Jerry --- poking harmless fun at each other! There, she was coming, I heard her squeaky footsteps from the doorway.

"Hello, welcome, home, Mandy, I have kept half a bottle of lemonade for you --- as I couldn't finish the whole bottle! She raised her eyebrows, much to my delight, and slowly replied "yes, I have also got half a chocolate for you 'because I couldn't eat: it is a sea-salt chocolate"! And we both laughed. She hugged me, I petted her hair and off she ran to the washroom --- for a quick shower, saying, please keep a cup of coffee on the gas for me. Shall come out soon from the washroom" and she disappeared from the doorway, I rushed to the kitchen to make coffee for her and some light snacks – mixture of cookies, nuts, chips and soup sticks--- our favorite evening nick naks.

As always, we discussed the day's happenings, in the balcony, sipping coffee and eating the snacks in between. I was eager to tell her about Cathy's brother—Roland—and observe her reaction to my talk. I told her about Gilbert, how Gilbert side stepped on the name of Roland, and said he too is staying in the same building as Cathy's building. Also, I told her how Cathy was grumpy on the school bus and how she had an argument with Meera, our classmate. I added I did not like Cathy's behavior today, as she did not talk to me and appeared sulky. I paused for Mandy's input, but she did not take any interest and appeared silent. "Anky, take the day as it comes, see all, hear all, and that's it. Do not take outside pressure on you" I loved my sister for her wise talks! And how was your day, Mandy "All OK"? "NO", not Okay, Mandy replied. My bosses' son returned very late at home, and my Boss gave him a thrashing, and his mood was off--- he was sympathetic and yet offended --- at his son's behavior. Amrit Lal Shah, my boss, was a cool and calm man. He called his wife and was blaming her for his son's misdeeds. Because our office is small, we can hear everyone's talk on the mobile. Hence, all our office was gloomy today. "How big is his son, you have an idea, Mandy? "Yes" my boss said Sudesh was nineteen years old—

soon he will be no longer a teenager, and this is the age where mind gets corrupted. Mandy had a sympathetic look, yet her face seemed to be stern. "Looks like, Mandy, you are upset, Is it so? "Yes", I am upset because my boss is quite a good man and despite his goodness: his home situation is like that? Though it is none of our staff concern, it sets a gloom in the office atmosphere, and I am thinking of changing my job". I am trying to get a job in the fitness industry, which job is closer to my heart. Mandy ended her talk. M A N D Y …. Did I not tell you Gilbert has a place available, and YOU can straight away open a private Fitness Class. "Sounds very good, you can take Cathy, Gilbert, myself as your first students: here is a brother wishing success in your new proposed venture. Cheers! And we suddenly embraced each other!

Chapter 8

The New Venue

Weekends are pleasurable. We all love it; in fact, we crave it. Once the Monday Blues are over, and we are on Tuesday, we start mentally counting now only 3 days more, and Friday evening is regaled to a mighty vision: parties, dances, dinner, outings and what not. Every individual is different, yet the mind also looks for relaxing the bodies on holidays—be it weekend or holiday of any sort. This time, I was thinking about going out with Mandy, Cathy and her brother, Roland--- if it materializes. And where could the Venue be? Mentally, we, as friends, like to go Dutch--- so it is not a burden on anyone. In that way, there will be a fair share policy of expending on the food bill. However, my BOSS, Mandy, would be the decision maker – or else if Roland has any say in it. The phone rang, displaying an unknown number. Hesitantly, I picked up the call: "Need Mandira to talk to me, I am Sudesh, my dad told me to call her: she works for our office: Janta Imports and Exports. There was a pause and again the gruff voice said "to whom am I speaking, please. "My name is Ankesh, and I am Mandira's brother" I replied softly. By this time, hearing the phone ring, Mandy had already come to the telephone stand. Closing the mouthpiece with my hand, I told Mandy, softly: One Mr. Sudesh is on the line. Mandy was surprised yet took the phone from my hand and said "Yes, this is Mandira, how can I help you, Sudesh? After a brief pause, Sudesh replied: My dad, is not well, he requested me to inform you, if you could come tomorrow to office early and take the office keys from his driver, Ratan Lal, from the office parking lot at 8am. This is a special request from my dad, since I must take him to the hospital. "Okay, Sudesh, done, I shall be at the office parking lot at 8 am... what is the vehicle number and the color of the vehicle, please send me on my WhatsApp --- your dad has my number, and she hung up. Mandy looked into my eyes and said "I don't think my employer will let me go easily, even if I give him a resignation letter tomorrow. "He trusts me, respects my work, and looks upon me as his daughter: he never gets angry on me, though he shouts at others sometimes. As a mark of loyalty, I will obey his request, Mandy ended the conversation. "Mandy, everyone likes you, because you are *my* sister... and I looked lovingly at her. Anky took a piece of my credit for himself! I cajoled him by tickling his ribs. There was another call and without thinking, I handed over the phone to Mandy. "Thank You So Much, Mandira, I have already sent you details on your mobile: it was my boss: Amrit Lal Shah. I wanted to ask by boss about his health, but he had already closed his phone.

I turned towards the kitchen to wash the coffee mugs and the plates. I realized Mandy had not finished her coffee as she had been talking on the phone, I called out "Mandy, are you donating your half cup of coffee to the kitchen sink? There is still a chance for you to drink it now, or else, the sink will thank you. She came running behind me and pulled the tray from my hands, saying "I shall finish my coffee and wash the dishes, you can go and play on your computer, if you need to", else continue sitting in the balcony, shall join you after some time. Again, the phone rang: it was Cathy, and she was glad to talk to me. "Why were you so sulky the other day, Cathy? What happened? "It was my brother, Roland, who shouted at me in the morning as I had eaten his cupcake thinking it was for me. I remembered this incident and became sulky. Sorry for the annoyance, Ankesh! "It is OK with me, Cathy, I did not know all this, but why did you bring that memory late in the afternoon? "Because Roland is a bit short tempered, and when I saw you, I remember how good you are with Mandira --- and I suddenly felt emotional. Forget it, Ankesh. "OK, now you are OK, say, what did you call me for? ""Ankesh, we would love to meet you and Mandira, my brother was asking what the venue could be?" "Cathy, I can't decide, we will leave it to you guys, shall also have a word with my sister. Please decide and call later---Mandy is in the kitchen. Who is Mandy?" Oh! That is my sister's name: I call her Mandy, to the world she is M-a-n-d-i-r-a. "How nice, I like that name MANDY." ---give her my regards, shall call you later, bye for now. And she hung up.

Mandy, where are you? Cathy had called, she wanted to ….."Just a minute" Mandy replied from the corridor, I am hanging clothes, shall join you in your room, in about five minutes time. I went to my room, and sat at the computer table, opened the unit to check any mails had come in. Yes, there was one from Dad... they had booked their tickets to Mumbai on 30th of November. What a delight! And it was a

Friday evening….. "Mandy, Mandy, please come here fast ---Mom and Dad are arriving in Mumbai on 30ᵗʰ November. As my voice was quite loud, Mandy came rushing in my room, and she saw me pointing on the computer screen: See this mail, our parents are coming on 30ᵗʰ November, which is a Friday!! Mandy too was overjoyed--- she kissed the computer screen, and then rotated her hand on my head. "Anky, Anky, this is the best news we got. By that time, I was typing on the keyboard …….WELCOME, WELCOME, WELCOME….WE ARE OVERJOYED. Thank You mom and dad… we are really, really excited, excited……. LOVES,LOVES, ME AND MANDY.

After about five minutes, I calmed down and told Mandy about Cathy's call. She also was of the opinion, since Cathy and Roland were deciding for the treat, let them suggest the venue. The phone rang again. It was Cathy. I turned the call on conference line so Mandy too could hear: "Hello, Ankesh and Mandira, my brother Roland has suggested "WONGKIN the Chinese restaurant at MARRIOT, PALI HILL. We replied, "YES OK" and thanked her and put off the phone. ONLY THEN WE REALISED WE HAD A BAD INCIDENT IN THAT HOTEL.

Chapter 9

Tail Tell Tales

Mandy was staring at her phone piece. It was nearly eight o'clock, and she was in the parking lot, waiting for Ratan Lal, the driver of Janata Imports and Exports. In the busy city area, it was uncomfortable with all passersby staring at her. Then she saw a pickup with "Janata Imports and Exports" written on its body. The road was too congested area for Ratan Lal to make a "U" turn and come towards her. On an impulse, she dashed around the curve, and managed to signal the driver, by showing her hand. Ratan Lal caught her hand's image in his side mirror and horned twice to let her know she could take office keys while he put his vehicle on hazard mode. Ratan Lal dangled his arm on the vehicle window so that Mandira could grab the keys and go to the office. With a sweep of her right hand Mandira grabbed the keys from the driver. Misson accomplished, she waved her hand to the driver and entered the staircase of the office building. She opened the office door, switched on the lights and called Sudesh on his mobile. Sudesh recognized the number and immediately politely said "Good Morning, me and papa are in the hospital now. The doctor will see him in ten minutes time, shall call you after 30 minutes. I got busy with paperwork, meantime the other two employees, Pawar, and Shrikant arrived together, wishing me *"Namaste"* —an Indian way of greeting. I too replied *"Namaste"* to them.

Pawar informed me, Sudesh had called him yesterday, informing him dad was not well. It was enough to inform Pawar as sure enough, Pawar would inform Shrikant, I concluded in my mind. As courtesy sake, Pawar called for tea from the café downstairs and handed me the tea in a glass --- customary in this part of the world.

Office calls were being answered by Shrikant, and I was busy doing my job — checking emails, replying to urgent ones, with a "CC" to the boss and concerned staff. Munshi, the accountant just arrived in the office, wishing *"Namaste Ji"* to all. My cell rang and it was Sudesh online "Mam nothing much to worry, Papa just requires some rest, his BP is slightly high, rest all OK. The Dr. has advised him to take 3 days' rest. I am now going back to my home, along with Papa. Here is Papa, he wants to speak to you. "Hello, hello, Sir, what happened suddenly to you" I echoed with a little heaviness in my voice. "Hello, *Beti*, (daughter) how are you? Sorry, I gave you trouble in the morning, to open the office, as you are the nearest staff near our office. "No, worries, Sir, my pleasure to help you". I replied politely and added "Please take rest, you will be alright soon. Shall pray for your good health." I could imagine the old man, walking slowly with a stick, and Sudesh by his side.

The day became long, with the boss not in! I skipped the evening classes and decided to go to the K Club instead. On my way back to home, I decided to buy some chicken cutlets and spring rolls for our supper. Anky always loves outside food, with a confession: So, do I.

Reaching home, I quickly changed my dress, ready to go to K Club for a practice session. By the time I would return, Anky would have finished his homework and evening tea. So, I was free to some extent to indulge in my favorite past time. Sports! I left a note for Anky, informing him, I shall be home by 7 PM.

K Club was only fifteen minutes away, yet I paced quickly, so I can enjoy at least sixty minutes of peaceful karate and boxing practice. My regime was quite serious, and I spared no time for gossip with gym mates. Only a small "Hi" was enough to get by, that too, for a courtesy sake. The Boxing Corner was empty to my good fortune, and I wore my gloves and started punching the sandbag. One, Two, Three, Ho, Ho, and I went on and on for thirty minutes straight. Beads of perspiration were spreading on my arms, and I took my hand towel and wiped off the sweat. From the windowsill, I could see many passersby going here and there, since it was a one-way vision glass pane. I clearly noticed a tall guy deliberating making rounds near the windowsill. I still had the comfort of watching and not being watched! Game over, I moved to the Judo pitch: it was full, yet a kind soul, backed out, and allowed me to take a position in the ring. I saluted her and went to the inner arena for free practice. A young lady, by the name, Gaily, with curly hair, offered to play Judo with me. I was delighted to find a partner, and we started playing, first, making a deep bow as a respect to the practice. My opponent was terrific, she lounged at me from a short distance and tried to uplift my legs and throw me on the ground! Her efforts failed as I had a good height compared to her stature and, instead, I grounded her in a jiffy. She rose with a lightning speed and again tried to play the same act, but again failed as I had spun my right leg and was about to hit her a deadly blow, and in time withdrew my leg spin, least she gets hurt terribly. She bowed and waved a "Bye" yet turned to ask me if I was an instructor here! Upon my negative reply, she thanked me and quit silently. Unknowingly, many pairs of eyes were watching us silently--- until we heard a few claps. My day was done. I picked up my things and walked to my residence, eager to see Anky. On way out, I saw Cathy sitting near the pond—perhaps, waiting for her brother!

Anky was already in the kitchen making coffee. He turned around and said "Mandy, what are these goodies you have brought? Are they for now or for supper?" "Darling, we can have a bit later, after I finish my wash-up. Is that OK with you? Mandy said to me. In the meantime, check if there are any emails saying so, she disappeared. I had already checked my mailbox, and there was none, except some junk emails, which I deleted. Having nothing more to do, I arranged the centre piece table in the balcony, laid down a mat and brought out coffee mugs and snacks. I seated myself at the far end of balcony, from where I could get a bird's eye view of the city. Mandy joined me, looking fresh and relaxed. We sipped our coffee asking each other, how the day was. The accompanying snacks were nice, and we relished every crumb of it. "Anky", my Boss did not come to the office today. He is sick, in fact, I collected the office keys from Ratan Lal, the company driver and was quite busy in the office throughout the day. My boss spoke to me from the hospital and said he won't be coming to office for three days--- yeah, I am going to be busy the next three days or so. "Do you want any help in the office? I quipped in, knowing very well her answer. She nodded her head, saying" yes, I wish you could, but you got your school to go to--- remember that. And we laughed. Mandy added "my office colleagues were feeling a bit **J** (jealous) as they know my boss favors me a lot" I heard a crude discreet remark –they said, the Boss could me make me the GM of the company some day! *They do not know I want to quit the company as soon as possible"* Mandy replied gently.

"OK, let us think about the invitation of Cathy and her brother: Do we go or decline? I asked Mandy. Mandy said to me:

Something is telling me Roland is the same person who teased me by calling "RED.RED. RED. He was a regular at Marriot's' He is tall. He did not attend our meeting, though he confirmed earlier, as per Cathy's words. Still, we saw him escorting Cathy. Also, Cathy was saying her brother is short tempered. He shouted at his sister and made her cry early in the morning. Roland is the culprit. Today, in the K Club I saw him while I was doing my work outs. He deliberately crossed my path and called me "Mandira" ---but I did not turn my head to look at him----- he saw my name in the Club Register, wherein I had signed to enter the club. He followed me and jotted down his name below my name but did not do any workouts, as he was glancing at me through the screened windows of the club.

I was quite upset after listening to my sweet sister mANDY. She is in my name and in my life. I will stop talking to CAThy. *I hate her now*. And she wants some training from you!

The telephone rang. I saw Cathy's cell number. I picked up the call but did not answer. My silence declined their invitation. Mandy danced round and round, true to her name, as my granny had said She is like a *Mandira* --- a kitchen tool used for mashing and churning curds into *lassi* (butter milk)

Again, the telephone rang. We both did not want to pick up the line. But as the ring was constantly going on, I picked up the call. "Hello, young man, Ankesh, you not around in the house?" It was our Uncle Jerry. I apologized for the delayed pick-up of the call. "Never mind, you and Mandira at home?" "Yes, very much, we both are at home, Uncle. "I have a few things in my car, shall drop by in ten minutes, is it OK? "Most welcome, Uncle" and the line went dead. Mandy was listening to the conversation but did not intervene as it was a brief call. "Do you think, it is a good idea to tell him about Cathy and Roland? I inquired of my sister. "No, need to open old wounds" it may even reach our parents! "Mandy you are very wise. How I wish I could be so straight forward in thinking, like you." "One day, you will, my pet"

Mandy replied to me instantly. It brought comfort to both of us. and we heard the bell ring. It was Uncle Jerry. "Good evening", and Welcome Sherry, you are so loving, and what is this big crate? "It is Alphonso mangoes: a client of dad's gave us two crates--- so Dad thought about you two. I know we all love mangoes. Dad's car is on hazard, quick I am leaving now. One more thing, there is a surprise party at our place coming weekend. Be at our place by 6pm----- till then keep on checking your WhatsApp messages –shall send you the invitation". Mandy pulled out two bottles of water, "for you and Uncle", and Mandy placed the two bottles in her hands. Sherry accepted and said Bye, we waved at her, and she too waved back saying "Bye for now".

Uncle is a nice generous person. He always keeps in touch with us--- he has many rich business contacts and many times he receives gifts from his clients, sometimes even from overseas. Remember, last time he brought us nice date chocolates--- Choco-dates and some *Baklava* –gulf specialties. And what are they celebrating next weekend, any idea? Anky. "You should know better, you were born before me," Anky replied, laughing over his own statement. Mandy appeared somewhat dazed, but cleverly replied, oh, yes, I remember and abruptly stopped. "Tell me no, tell me, please, Anky pleaded. "Yes, they may be celebrating Halloween Day! "No, no, that is over, last week was Halloween. "Honestly, I don't know myself, can't guess," Mandy replied. "OK, let us eat some mangoes--- yes MAN--GO- and I picked one big mango, went to the kitchen and cut in four big slices, with a circular cut along the mango seed. I took one slice and the big round seed, but Mandy cut one slice in two and gave it to me. We both could not finish the full mango and kept two slices back in the fridge.

We were both feeling sleepy. Mandy informed me, she will go to her office a little late as Sudesh will pick her up in his car and deposit her in the office. She had already sent Sudesh her location details. Happy with the arrangements, we both went to see romantic stories on Amazon Kindle. We searched for romantic tales on Google and Amazon Kindle. Among the new books released, was a Best Seller: "A Leaf Has Life" by Suresh Thadhani. There was a nice cover page on that book of a lady standing on a boat with her hair flowing in the breeze. We selected that book and enjoyed the story end to end. The story lasted for forty-five minutes, and Mandy promised to see more stories by the same author.

With romantic dreams, the approaching Christmas, and our parents' arrivals, in our mind, we went to sleep.

Chapter 10

The Queen Reigns

Mandy woke me up…."Anky ! It is 6 o'clock , hurry up, rush for bath and breakfast, else you will be late for school. "And why aren't you dressed up, Mandy. "I told you Sudesh will come today to pick me up to drop me at the office. You forgot? "Oh! Mandy, can he also drop me at school, please? I love a car drive! "I hardly know him; it would be foolish to take liberties with strangers. Uneasily, I got up to get ready and go to school. Yes, Mandy is right, I consoled myself. Yet, I imagined a short scene of my being driven on a long beach road, by Uncle Jerry, perhaps. I could hear the school bus horning below our building. Quickly, I pulled the school bag on my shoulder, said "Bye" to Mandy and left for the school bus. I was on time and the conductor pushed me into the bus and gently closed the bulky door.

I was in no mood to crane my neck for Cathy, in fact, I happened to sit next to Gilbert. We wished "Good Morning" to each other and that was the only conversation we had. We alighted from the bus in a single file stream and went to our respective classes.

The Science teacher, Mrs. Fatima, was a jolly good teacher. She would crack little jokes or pull someone's leg and make the class lighter. Furthermore, Science, as a subject was everyone's favorite and we all had good vibes during this period. Today, we were learning about water purification and means of filtration. Jimmy raised his hand and said his kidneys have filtered the water in his body and he wanted to go the toilet. There was hysterical laughter in the class and the bell rang and the period was over. School days are fun, and most of the children mingled without reservations, I felt.

The next few periods like geography, history, and arithmetic were well attended to. There was a relief when lunch time neared. Today, I had not brought any lunch and thought of skipping it and checking my mobile cell for any messages. I saw an empty school bench in the playground area and went there. The day was getting darker, there was a nice breeze and there could be light showers, I imagined. Sitting on the bench I ran through my WhatsApp messages. Yes, there was one from Sherry "Excited to announce a lovely evening party at my residence, this weekend, at 6pm. --- cc to Mandira. "Sherry was very good at making us laugh and this was one of the ways she would keep us entertained…. By half messages at intervals, like today's message. Good One, I mentally remarked, will discuss with Mandy, in the evening.

The climate was changing from sunny to cloudy, and again from cloudy to hot and sultry. Usually during this period of "ber" months (September, October, November, and December), climate is varying and I loved these months. This period had many holidays, and I loved the changing seasons. There was still the excitement of the weekend outing at Uncle Jerry's house as well as the approaching month of December when our parents would be here.

On approaching home, the first thing I did was go for a bath and freshen up myself. Probably, today's weather was not suiting me, as I felt I could be heading for a Flu. I prayed to God, I should keep well as I was eager to attend the party at my uncle's place at Santa Cruz area, near Mumbai Airport. Yes, this was another reason I wanted to go to his apartment, as I could watch the planes landing and take-off! A sight to behold any time of the day! As I came out of the washroom, I heard the opening of the latch and Mandy arrived with a huge bunch of flowers. "What is this for, Mandy? I asked. "Nothing, no worries--- these flowers were received by my Boss in the hospital. He received too many flowers, his ward was overfull, so to speak. Hence, Sudesh brought it for me, insisting I take it, as per his father's advice. So, kind of him.

Also, one more thing, I too want to visit my Boss, and Sudesh had confirmed to me, he can come to our place and pick me up. And I told him I would visit the hospital, bringing my brother--- and that is you: she pointed her long index finger towards me. I was happy and retorted: Mandy, my wish has come true: I wanted someone to take me for a drive to a beach--- and Beach Candy Hospital is on Beach Road! God is Great! "Mandy, I shall make a strong coffee for you, along with a mini boiled egg sandwich and then we shall sit in the balcony and discuss other things --- and he winked at me – giving me a hint of strange WhatsApp messages! In the meantime, please go and freshen up. I shall find a place for the bouquet --- near Lord Budha's statue.

I made strong coffee, egg sandwich and for myself took some chips and biscuits from the jars. When Mandy sat on her chair, I pulled out my mobile and showed her the message received from Sherry: "Excited to announce a lovely evening party at my residence, this weekend, at 6pm. --- cc to Mandira. "

But this is **Not** the message I received on my cell; Mandy replied. The message I have received is: "A feast of Chicken Biryani, without Chicken, but with mixed vegetables". How funny! And she fooled me, by saying "CC" to you. How Clever of Sherry!

Mandy, what could be the feast about? Is she getting married? Or is it Uncle Jerry's Birthday? "Let's not guess further, we should wait for her next message---- probably it will be the last one …… as in the evening, it will be the "feast". So, let us wait.

We were both tired and decided to sleep early. Also, Sudesh will be coming tomorrow to pick us up by Nine O' clock. We bade good night to each other and went to our respective rooms. Sleep evaded me for a long time. Did Sherry know about

Cathy, as she referred to as "Tiny Cathy"? And why be so mysterious about a "feast". Anyway, I tried to forget about that for now, and rather thought about the Beach drive awaiting tomorrow. Another thing struck me: It seemed my sister's Boss loved Mandy. Although my sister was working part -time with him, he relied more on her than on others? And would he allow her to leave the office, if she resigned. I did not know much about office and office work, but there was an uncanny feeling that the Boss was relying on Mandy more than the other staff! Also, Sudesh was his son, why did he insist Sudesh could drop and pick us up instead of his company driver? These were baffling questions for my little head to understand, so I pulled the blanket and closed my eyes.

When I opened my eyes around seven o" clock, I could hear Mandy prancing about in the kitchen. She must be practicing boxing, wearing gloves, I guessed. Once, Mandy told me she takes gloves even to her office as she feels connected to me! I always Thanked God for giving me a loving and a very caring sister. She was my everything, I could honestly confess. "Creamy iced Tea will do today, for you, Anky? Mandy whispered from the doorway. I knew Mandy always had good ways to get me out of the bed--- even on weekends, because she was a Sun Riser! "Yes, for a change, I shall have it" I joked with her, knowing fully well I was lying. "So be it, order of Potato Sandwich and French fries stands cancelled "Mandy uttered from the gangway. "Oh No, Mandy don't cancel any orders early in the morning, for your one and only one customer…..and I hopped from my bed and rushed to the wash room.

Mandy's cell phone rang and I heard her …… ending sentence, yes "we will come down the stairs at nine o'clock no worries. Mandy's Boss was orderly, and he had told Sudesh to abide by the timings and go and pick up Mandy from her home at nine o'clock! I looked at the clock, it was just 7.30am, lots of time still, I said in my mind.

Mandy was busy making extra coffee, and she had gathered some fruits from the fridge for the hospital visit. She poured the extra coffee in a thermos flask and some chips and biscuits for Sudesh, in a separate bag. Clever of her, Mandy was quite thoughtful.

"Anky, sit this side (pointing left) of the table, you can have your coffee and the sandwich I have made and bring the laptop to check mail. I am sitting beside you so we can read the mail together. It will save time as we need to be ready before 9 am. "Got it, shall bring the laptop, and we watched the screen go ready. There was no mail, but our cell phones rang together! There was a message from Sherry: Good Morning, Remember, 6pm the show begins, I have a little crown for Miss Tiny Cathy. Bring Your Own Drinks, ample of snacks SANS drinks! Take Away Gifts Ready for Early Birds" Loves, Sherry" Always, a funny interesting message from Sherry!

At sharp 8.55am we were at the car parking lot. We noticed a light blue BMW 6868 MAH car on a hazard. A window lowered and Sudesh waved out his hand welcoming us. Mandy sat in the front seat, and me on the back seat, while uttering "Good Morning, Sudesh" Sudesh too wished us Good Morning and he drove the car. We were fascinated by the interiors of the car, light blue décor, a small TV screen in the back seat, and plenty of leg room. We were lucky to get such a car-ride early in the morning, but of course for the wrong reason: visiting Mandy's Boss in the Breach Candy Hospital! "This is Ankesh, my one and only brother, a school going kid" Mandy introduced me to Sudesh. And glancing at me, Mandy said "Anky, this is Sudesh, son of my Boss, a fine gentleman. I shook hands with Sudesh, my tiny hand felt like making a handshake with a giant: I also handed to Sudesh the coffee flask and chips and biscuits. He only accepted the coffee and poured a glass to drink before driving the vehicle. He thanked us for the good thought of bringing coffee. He said, "Any time is Coffee time is Mine Time" and chuckled. Sudesh was very tall, broad shouldered and quite fair. "Nice to meet you, Ankesh, Sudesh replied, looking in his rear mirror and talking to my reflection in the mirror. "How is your dad faring now?" *Didi*" (sister, in Indian language) he is much better now. Thank God. I noticed his voice trembled a little, like as if he was sobbing." Is anything the matter, Sudesh, are you alright? For a long time, Sudesh was silently driving, concentrating on the huge traffic. This patch of road was quite bad for traffic, as it was the only road linking to Worli Sea face: ahead was a clearer road to Breach Candy with four lanes, and where you could get a panoramic view of Mumbai's coastline. Anky was busy watching and enjoying the drive. At last, Sudesh said in a soft voice" *Didi*, papa is short tempered and me and him have a constant argument whenever I have a holiday from the college. In fact, much of the blood pressure he accumulates is due to our own family faults--- he does not like high volume of TV. My mom is hard of hearing and if she cannot enjoy TV, she sulks. Also, I have a fault too, on weekends I return home late, and he does not like it. He will not sleep before I reach the house. Then he growls at me, and we have a clash of words, sometimes. I confess I am a social drinker, and he can *sense* when I am a little drunk…. he stopped on the sentence. And became sober again.

"Sudesh, may I ask you a question? Mandy politely asked Sudesh. Yes, *Didi*, go on I am listening. "You said, sometimes, you drink a little. Can you manage to avoid drinks totally? It could solve one of your family problems. "I am trying to, *Didi*. But it is not easy, all my friends drink a little, even girls, enjoy drinking. OK, understood, I shall be firmer and control myself. "Do your people socialize – I mean, do they invite relatives, or friends to your place. "Yes, they do, but it is rare now as dad gets tired soon. Besides, he manages the business too, as you are aware. It also adds stress to his life. We were nearing the destination and Sudesh got a parking slot immediately. We went to ward 321 IC unit.

Looking at Amrit Lal Shah, I felt he was still weak. I greeted him politely, introducing him to my brother at the same time. We both shook hands with him, and he seemed to be pleased to see us. Near his bed, sitting across, there was lady wearing a light blue sari, and I guessed it she could be his wife. Amrit Lal lifted his finger, and pointing towards her, he told us: She was his *dharm patni,* (respected wife) Neelam. Anky and I went to her and shook hands and did a *Namaste. (folded hands)*

Amrit Lal ordered Tea for us through his intercom messaging. Sudesh, kept his hand on his dad's shoulder and said, 'Papa don't worry, I shall drop them home back, whenever they say so". Anky moved to the window to glance at the scene outside: huge waves were crashing on the corniche rocks and people were thoroughly enjoying the weather. Anky jumped up and whistled, forgetting he was in the hospital.

Amrit Lal thanked me for devoting more time in the office and missing my college studies. He said he had a plan for me, and would discuss it with me, once he resumes normal duties.

My Boss gave me an intense gaze, as if trying to recall something--- *and important it was Amrit Lal spoke silently and sweetly: She had come for an interview in my office, two years ago, for the* *post of an Accountant. Among the certificates and testimonials, she had shown me, there were more certificates in Sports --- Judo, Karate, Boxing, Swimming, Kick Boxing, Base Ball, Running, and what not. Always a Topper, never a Runner Up. At that time, I had a vision of her as an All-Rounder. **And True it was, And True IT IS.*** His eyes became moist.

I thanked him and assured him of my support, (though reluctantly said no inwardly.) Then, Amrit Lal made a surprising statement, looking pointedly at me "*Beti*, my son is a young athlete and is not interested in the type of my business. Suggest, if you two can help me open a sports club: you are an ace champion, and he too is an allrounder. I have the money and the means to start a new venture. I am thinking of closing my import export business. Think about it and please let me know. **I felt, as if, some stars had fallen in my lap!** I was so overjoyed! Sir, do you really mean it? I shall gladly go for it and produced my gloves from my handbag, wearing them and shaking my fists in the air. THIS IS MY TRUE VISION.

The tea arrived and we raised a toast! I requested Sudesh to leave us at our residence since we had an outing in the evening. Anky looked at my gloves and said, "Useful Gift", no one understood, except us. Then, Anky briefly informed of the unfortunate incidence that happened a week ago, in the Marriot Hotel, Bandstand, Bandra, pulling out the gloves from Mandy's purse and exhibiting proudly to everyone. Neelam let out a small scream.

The Head Sister of the hospital ward dropped in to see the patient. She said "Good Morning, Uncle how are you feeling today? "Oh! Much better than yesterday. I believe you have very good Doctors and Nursing here. They all took good care of me, and I am grateful to all staff here" replied Amrit Lal. "Thank You So Much for your good words: Kindly leave your comments while checking out. I suppose you are being discharged today evening. Dr. Mathews will let you know when he comes on his rounds now. She left the ward saying "Bye" to us. "We are ready to leave now, as we have household jobs for the weekend" I told to Sudesh, who was busy on his mobile. "Any time now is OK, but I suggest letting DR. Mathew see papa. He is due here any moment for his routine checkup. Precisely there was a tap on the door, and DR. Mathews popped in. "Good morning" Mr. Amrit Lal, and how are you feeling today? Dr. Mathews looked at the drip instrument and said "Good" your drip is over and be relaxed, sister will remove the needles now. No fever, No coughs, No loose motions, I suppose. Good, you can go home today evening, else if you prefer, you can stay one more night. On an impulse, Anky asked the doctor, Sir, do you feel sick anytime like we do? We all laughed, but the Doctor quietly replied, "Sunny, we are all humans, and we do tend to fall sick because of viruses in the air. Plus, it also depends upon your body resistance – some people are weak minded, and some are strong, like Sudesh, and this young lady, pointing to Mandira. The best medicine is fruits, healthy foods, and exercises. And Sunny, do you do any exercises? Yes, Sir, I do all my exercises what my teacher gives in the school" --making all of us laugh! " Clever boy", the doctor said, and he moved towards the door, signaling the sister to come and remove the patient's needles. Since the room became crowded, we signaled Sudesh to move. Papa, we are leaving now, and I shall drop Mandira and her brother, then buy the groceries and come here and Mama, do you want me to bring you anything from the supermarket? No, *Beta*, just come soon. "OK, see you and we waved to his parents --- reminding Amrit Lal to eat the fruits we had bought. On our way out, Amrit Lal called out

"Please, come to our house on next-to-next Sunday, as it is Sudesh's Birthday, and we shall all celebrate at our place. We said "Thank You very much, we shall come and Anky and me went to touch the feet of Sudesh's parents, for their Blessings, as is our Indian culture. We left on a happy note, Anky much relieved for a return car journey by the beach side. In the car, Sudesh asked me how I keep myself fit and fine. Anky poked in "Uncle come to our house and see the awards and gold medals my sister has won in many sports like, Judo, Karate, (both Black Belt Holder) Boxing, Swimming, and what else, Mandy—I keep on forgetting!" "Ghosh, you are a genius, *Didi*, I don't' think I can match you in merits…. I am a puppy before you. That statement made us laugh. OK, someday, we will meet in a sports club. "Didi, where do you practice your activities?" Sudesh asked me. "K Club" Bandra area" "Oh! I see" he just replied. "And you--- where do you go for your activities, Sudesh? "Me, I am a member of Bombay Gymkhana, Worli. It is one of the biggest sports clubs and has many good fitness trainers. I go only four times a week, due to time constraint. We were approaching our destination, and Sudesh left us just below our building, giving a hazard. We requested him to come up, but due to "no parking" he declined, saying "some other time" and we dispersed. Anky was very happy with the drive, and he held my hand, saying "I wish I could go again, sometimes. Nice views of the seashore.

We were a bit tired, and both of us decided to take a little nap before our evening outing.

Getting up at around 5pm, I rushed to Mandy to get up and get dressed, while I prepared a strong cup of coffee for both of us. I asked Mandy, what sort of gift we should carry for the mysterious occasion. Sherry had just written "Tiny Cat... I did not want to take her name, so I wrote only that much. Wait Mandy, I think I have guessed. Has Sherry got a pet cat? And is she small (tiny)? "No idea" Mandy replied. But I think you are right, as far as we know, we know, Sherry is the only child Uncle Jerry has. His wife died at childbirth and Uncle Jerry has been a doting father. Anyway, instead of giving them a gift, shall we carry the bouquet of fresh flowers we received from Sudesh. "Lovely Idea", I said. And we both sat down together to add some flowers from our garden. I was quite artistic and knew very well to make garlands and flower bouquets. And I wrote a beautiful sentence:

To Tiny Cathy, With Our Good Wishes: Flowers Say Everything, At Every Occasion. Happy Tidings. From MANDYANDY. It looked so good, the huge bouquet with a beautiful card made by me from PRINTSHOP. And we took a Selfie, both of us smiling, and copied the image on our WhatsApp.

Mandy booked a cab for 5.30pm. We were all ready and set to go. The cab arrived. We reached in 20 minutes --- still ahead of time. We looked up at the illuminated villa. Yes, some music was also going on. We reached the staircase and heard lot of Meows, Meows, Meows. Sherry came running to us, saying TINY **Cathy** is her pet CAT. They were celebrating a litter of cats she had delivered just a week back. Every early bird, like us, could take away a **CAThy** as a gift from Sherry and Uncle Jerry. I put my hands on my ears—did not wanted to hear that name! We meowed and two little kittens meowed and came towards us. So Cute! Mandy replied and picked up one of the cats.... but I didn't. I don't like Cats. We gave Sherry the bouquet --- she was very, very pleased, calling Uncle Jerry and showing him our gift. Uncle Jerry looked at the Gift Card and read the wordings word by word. Sherry was hearing it too---- and they applauded us heartly. Other guests also saw our artwork and the beautiful flowers. We all danced in a chorus; the cats caged in a glass cage with a netted opening at the top of the glass cage. The gong went on for seven chimes, each gong honoring seven cats born to Tiny Cathy.

Game Over. Sherry announced everyone to proceed to the dining hall. Food Lids were opened by three cooks stationed on the veranda. A Fishy Feast for The Queen's Region. No drinks were served. Only Fish Soup. **NB: STRICTLY NO CATS ALLOWED.** *They are all sleeping after eating fishy food.*

www.ingramcontent.com/pod-product-compliance
Lightning Source LLC
Chambersburg PA
CBHW031310130726
47988CB00007B/2788